Copyright © 2003 Uitgeverij Clavis, Amsterdam - Hasselt
Dual language copyright © 2004 Mantra Lingua
First published in 2003 by Uitgeverij Clavis, Amsterdam - Hasselt
First dual language publication in 2004 by Mantra Lingua
All rights reserved
A CIP record for this book is available from the British Library.

Published by Mantra Lingua
5 Alexandra Grove, London N12 8NU
www.mantralingua.com

富路比的朋友

Floppy's Friends

Guido van Genechten

Chinese translation by Sylvia Denham

mantra

每一日放學後，
富路比都出外跟牠的朋友玩耍，
富路比的朋友有各種大小身型和顏色，
但是…

Every day, after school,
Floppy went out to play
with his friends.
Floppy's friends were all
sizes and colours but…

牠們只會跟與自己的
模樣相似的兔子玩。

they only ever played with the
rabbits who looked like them.

『我希望我們可以一齊玩，』
富路比想。

"I wish we could all play together,"
thought Floppy.

富路比首先走去跟白兔們玩
『不要掉胡蘿蔔』，

First Floppy ran to play don't-drop-the-carrot
with the white rabbits.

富路比在單腳跳時
也沒有將胡蘿蔔掉下來。

Floppy didn't drop the carrot once,
not even when he hopped on one leg.

富路比跟著便和灰兔們玩『放風箏』，
『高呀，高呀！』富路比唱著，『但小心落地啊。』

Next Floppy played fly-a-kite with the grey rabbits.
"Up, up and away!" chanted Floppy. "But watch your landing."

富路比接著與棕兔們玩『蛙跳』，
『跳得高，跳得過！』富路比唱著。

Then Floppy played leapfrog with the brown rabbits.
"Jump up and jump over!" chanted Floppy.

最後富路比跟黑兔們玩『火車』，
『我可以做司機嗎？』富路比問道，
『好吧，』黑兔們說，牠們記得上一次富路比
是在火車的中段，牠引致最大的火車失事！

Finally Floppy played trains with the black rabbits.
"Can I be the driver?" asked Floppy.
"Ok," said the black rabbits. They remembered the last time Floppy
was in the middle of the train, he caused the most enormous crash!

第二天中午時，有一隻孤獨的小兔子站在樹下，
牠不是白色的，也不是灰色的，牠不是棕色，
亦不是黑色，牠有棕色和白色的斑紋。
牠看著所有的兔子興高采烈在一起，
牠也希望能夠加入，可是牠是新來的，
牠不認識牠們，也不懂得牠們的玩意。

The next afternoon under a tree stood a lonely little rabbit.
He wasn't white and he wasn't grey. He wasn't brown and
he wasn't black. He was dappled brown and white.
He watched all the rabbits having fun and wished that he could join in.
But being new he didn't know anybody and he didn't know their games.

當富路比看到新來的兔子時，
牠走過去。『你好，我是富路比，
你叫什麼名字？』牠問道，
『森美，』那斑兔說道。
『過來一齊玩吧，』富路比說。
『但是我不知道怎樣玩
你們的遊戲，』森美說，
『沒問題，我教你，』富路比說。

When Floppy saw the new rabbit he
went over to him. "Hi, I'm Floppy.
What's your name?" he asked.
"Samy," said the dappled rabbit.
"Come and play," said Floppy.
"But I don't know how to play
your games," said Samy.
"Don't worry. I'll show you,"
said Floppy.

富路比教森美玩『不要掉胡蘿蔔』，
富路比把胡蘿蔔放到頭上後便跑，
『真好玩，』森美說。

Floppy showed Samy don't-drop-the-carrot.
Floppy put the carrot on his head and off he went.
"Cool," said Samy.

跟著便輪到森美了，牠把胡蘿蔔放到頭上，
『你看，很容易嘛！』富路比說。

Then it was Samy's turn. He put the carrot on his head.
"See, it's easy!" said Floppy.

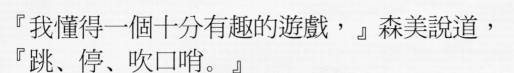

『我懂得一個十分有趣的遊戲，』森美說道，
『跳、停、吹口哨。』
『那是怎樣玩的？』富路比問道。
『你先跳，然後停，跟著吹口哨。噓噓！』
『真好玩啊』富路比笑道。

"I know a really cool game,"
said Samy, "skip-stop-whistle."
"How d'you play that?"
asked Floppy.
"You skip, stop and whistle:
WHEEEE!"
"Cool!" laughed Floppy.

其他兔子也來看看是什麼一回事，
『這是森美，』富路比說，
『森美，』一隻大兔子吃吃地笑道，
『牠應該叫做斑點啊。』
牠們都大笑，只有富路比
和森美例外。

The other rabbits came to see what was going on.
"This is Samy," said Floppy.
"Samy," giggled a big rabbit. "He should be called Spotty."
They all laughed, all except Floppy and Samy.

『斑點！斑點！森美是斑點！』
其他的兔子唱著。

"Spotty! Spotty! Sa-my is spo-tty!"
the other rabbits chanted.

『放一個胡蘿蔔風箏、蛙跳到火車、跳、
停、吹口哨。』
『那是怎樣玩的？』
那大兔子問道。

"Fly-a-carrot-kite-leapfrog-on-the-train
with a skip, stop and whistle."
"How d'you play that then?"
asked the big rabbit.

『你把胡蘿蔔放到你的頭上，然後放風箏，再蛙跳到火車上，跟著跳、停，接著吹口哨。噓噓！』
所有兔子都一齊參加玩森美這好玩的遊戲。

"Well," said Floppy. "You put a carrot on your head, fly-a-kite, leapfrog-on-the-train, skip, stop and whistle: WHEEEE!"
All the rabbits joined in Samy's cool game.

所有富路比的朋友都一齊玩！

And ALL Floppy's friends played together!